GILLY'S TOWER

GILLY'S TOWER

CONSTANCE SAVERY

Illustrated by
J. E. Niewenhuis

LUTTERWORTH PRESS
CAMBRIDGE

ISBN 0 7188 2280 3

Printed and bound in Great Britain by
Cox & Wyman Ltd, Reading

CONTENTS

CHAPTER

I

One Blue, Sunny Day

IT would never have happened if Gilly's brother Kildare had not thrown away an exercise-book that had some pages ruled for writing and others left blank for drawing pictures or maps. Only one page had been used.

Kildare threw the book away because he had stopped learning geography.

But it was a good book, much too good to be destroyed with the rest of the rubbish in Kildare's waste-paper basket. Gilly put it away in his play cupboard. One fine day in October he took it out and looked at it.

"I will write my life," said Gilly.

He tore out the used page. On the next page he wrote:

MY LIFE

By Gilbert Harcourt-Tudor

I am called Gilly for short, and I live on an island, Red Rocks, off the Welsh coast. Its Welsh name is Ynys Goch, and

the name of my home is Castell Goch or Red Castle.

Poppy and Kildare are my brother and sister. They are twins and rather old, and they go to a boarding-school. My other sister Jane and I go to school on the mainland: every day we go there by ferry-boat. Jane is nearly ten and I am seven plus.

Daddy's work often takes him and Mummy away for months. When they are not at home Auntie Enid takes care of us. She lives here. I have a very gentle white rabbit which I have named after Auntie Enid.

This term I am not to go to school because I was ill in the summer holidays, and the doctor says it will be better that I don't go to school till after Christmas. He said to Daddy that my brain is too active and must be given a rest.

I will now describe my illness, which

came about in this way. Daddy has a little cove under great cliffs, called Porth Grisial or Crystal Cove. There is a cave in it, Ogof Grisial. Jane and I were not allowed to go to Crystal Cove alone because the way to it was not safe; it could only be reached through a locked door and down a long flight of steep steps cut in the cliffside.

While Daddy and Mummy were away in Karambodia, Poppy and Kildare lent Crystal Cove to friends of theirs who wanted to build a huge rocket without asking leave from the police. They were three brothers. One was the same age as Poppy and Kildare, but the other two were grown-up, though young. It was a great secret, which Jane and I were not allowed to know.

So we searched till we found another key to fit the door. Then we went down the steps by ourselves. It was the day before the rocket was ready to be launched.

When we saw the rocket Jane screamed and ran away, calling to me to come too. But I am sorry to say I didn't. I went close up to have a look.

I do not remember what happened next. People tell me I must have meddled with the rocket, so perhaps I did. It blew up the cave and the steps and me. I was blown nearly into the sea. Kildare and another friend of his, Jack Osmond, and a team of men rescued me. Kildare fell and broke his arm. The police were angry. They made Poppy's and Kildare's friends pay a lot of money for a punishment. It was called a fine. . . .

Here Gilly grew tired of writing his *Life*, and he thought he would draw a picture of himself being blown up by the exploding space-rocket. He was enjoy-

ing his work very much when Auntie
Enid came in.

"Oh, Gilly, indoors again on such a
blue, sunny day!" she said. "I thought
you were digging in your garden, which
badly needs weeding. The doctor said
you must spend all your time in the open
air at present. Yes, yes, put away your
books like a good boy."

Gilly did not wish to leave off painting
the orange and scarlet flames of the
explosion. He argued and protested until
Daddy came in. No one could have been
less like a white rabbit than Daddy.

"Out you go, Gilly!" said Daddy.
"And mind you don't come back till
dinner-time!"

Gilly had to obey. But he did not
weed his untidy garden or go down to
play on the open shore beyond Crystal
Cove. Instead, he strolled down some of
the twisty lanes of little Red Island.

Presently he came to a round tower with a heap of ruins behind it.

This brown stone tower had stood in its place for hundreds of years before Gilly was born. Though still sound and weatherproof, it had a crumbling look of age under its thick cloak of ivy and moss. Jane and Gilly thought it was like the tower in a book of poems belonging to their father. One poem said:

". . . from yonder ivy-mantled tower
    The moping owl does to the moon complain
Of such as, wandering near her secret bower
    Molest her ancient solitary reign . . ."

Often the tower remained empty for many months; but from time to time it was occupied by an old artist who painted sea-pictures. He would drive up to the tower in a high, old-fashioned car, out of which came a sleeping-bag, a kettle, a frying-pan, some crockery, an easel, canvases, and paints. Taking a key from his pocket, he would unlock the door and go in.

The artist was not there that morning. A small furniture van stood near the door, which was wide open. Two men were bringing out a number of un-finished pictures.

A Tower of His Very Own

GILLY watched the men putting a bookcase, a desk, and an antique chair into the van. This done, the driver climbed into his seat.

"Isn't Mr. Black ever coming back again?" asked Gilly.

"No, he's packed it in," the driver answered. "He's eighty-three, too old for tramping round the world with his little paint-box.—Come on, Bill!" he shouted to the other man, who was still inside the tower. "We've got everything that was down on our list for us to take, haven't we? The old bloke said, leave the rest, he hadn't room for it."

Bill came on.

"Oh yeah, I only wanted a look-see from the top of the tower," said Bill; "but I wasn't going to trust my weight to

the ladder up there. We've finished, sure enough. Finny, as the French say. Gee up, mate."

He jumped into the cab and waved a good-bye to Gilly. The van lumbered off.

This was a good time to explore the ruins. Gilly explored them. When he came back, he saw something that he had not expected to see.

The key was still in the door.

Bill had forgotten it.

Or he had not troubled to take it away.

Like Bill, Gilly went to have a look-see.

The tower had only one room on the ground-floor; it was part kitchen, part sitting-room. In it were two shaky chairs, a dresser, a table, and a flat tin bath hanging on the wall. Dustpan and brush lay in a corner. Spiders had woven webs across the windows.

A wooden staircase took Gilly up to the one bedroom, and then to a kind of storeroom above it.

The bedroom was empty. In the storeroom a ladder showed the way to the roof.

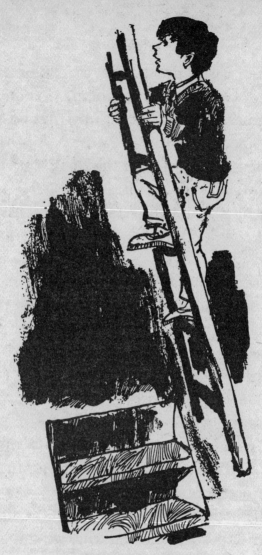

A ladder showed the way to the roof

Gilly shook the ladder and decided that it would bear his weight though it wouldn't bear Bill's. But the trap-door bolt was so heavy and rusty that he put off trying to move it until he had the help of Jane.

Going downstairs he sat on the dusty table, thinking about something he had heard his father say.

Nobody knew who owned the tower. Long ago there had been disputes among several people over the ownership; but the question had never been settled, and for many years the tower remained unoccupied. When Mr. Black moved in it was supposed that he must have a right to be there—but nobody quite liked to ask who gave him that right! Daddy had called him "a squatter".

"Well," said Gilly, when he had come to the end of his thinking, "one thing is quite clear. This tower does not belong to anybody now, so I shall take it for myself. Only, of course, I shall share it with Jane."

He walked out of the tower, locked the door, and took the key. "I don't believe," he said, "that there is another boy living who has a tower of his very own!"

Gilly ran all the way back to Red Castle. But when he burst into the house, eager to tell his wonderful news, he was surprised and disappointed to find only Auntie Enid at home. Daddy had been called unexpectedly to London for some days, and Mummy had gone with him.

Although he was longing to talk about his tower, it seemed wiser not to speak of it to Auntie Enid, who might have half a dozen reasons against his claiming the tower for his own. They would not be good reasons, Gilly was sure of that.

So he said nothing to her, though never

in his life had he found it so hard to hold his tongue. And Auntie Enid, for her part, was surprised when Gilly darted out of doors as soon as the mid-day meal was over without having to be told.

Jane would be returning from school by the four o'clock ferry-boat; but there was much to be done before he went down to the landing-stage to meet her and bring her in triumph to the tower.

He borrowed a broom and a yellow duster from the kitchen on his way out, much to the astonishment of Mrs. Pugh, who had come with a basket of fresh fish for sale.

"Now what would Gilly be wanting with a broom, whateffer?" she said to herself. "Neffer before have I seen a boy with a duster."

Gilly worked hard all the afternoon, sweeping and dusting and clearing away rubbish from the three rooms; but he did

Much to the astonishment of Mrs. Pugh

not clean the windows because he did not like to disturb the spiders. They had made such careful webs! Besides, the tower had belonged to them long before it belonged to him.

3

Jane Takes a Hand

AT four o'clock Gilly was waiting by the landing-stage, feeling pleased.

Jane and a dozen schoolfellows skipped off the ferry. At sight of Gilly, they giggled.

"Oh, Gilly!" cried Jane, "what HAVE you done to yourself? You're as black as a crow! And that new pullover that Auntie Enid made you—it's ruined!"

For the first time Gilly looked down at himself—and did not like what he saw. "Oh, never mind me!" he said. "I've got something important to show you. Come on!"

The other children were not coming

his way. They stared after him and Jane, still giggling.

Arrived at the tower, he unlocked the door and flung it open for Jane to enter.

"There!" he said. "What do you think of that? My tower!—my own tower! And yours. We always share, don't we?"

Jane was so delighted that at first she

could not speak. Then she caught Gilly's hands, and they danced round and round and round till they flopped on the floor for tiredness.

They danced round and round and round

"But I don't understand, Gilly," said Jane. "How does the tower come to be yours? Did Mr. Black give it to you? I thought it didn't really belong to him. He didn't and it didn't? Then how——? Please explain."

Gilly explained.

"Do you think," said Jane, "that it is ours for ever? That in our prayers to-night we ought to thank God for our lovely tower? Because we couldn't thank Him, could we, if it belonged all the while to someone else?"

"It can't belong to anyone else," said Gilly, "because Daddy said that it could only belong to one of the people who claimed it—and all the rest weren't telling the truth or perhaps had made a mistake. And the judges said none of them were to have it. Nobody else has claimed it for forty years. Only tramps slept there sometimes before Mr. Black came."

Jane was satisfied.

"Everybody who wanted it must be dead by now," she said. "We'll come down after tea and do some more cleaning. Oh, the windows!—they can't wait! Gilly, you dreadful boy, how could you leave the windows in such a mess?"

Jane seized a nasty little black rag that had once been a fine yellow duster. She had no kind thoughts about spiders. Whoosh went the duster!—and the spiders scuttled for their lives.

After that they ran home to tea.

Auntie Enid did not ask any questions. Gilly, she supposed, had been routing about in the loft over the woodshed—and she was well used to his looks after an hour up there. But she could hardly believe her eyes when she saw him rushing out of doors again as soon as tea was over.

"Why, what a remarkable thing!" said she. "He hasn't opened a book all day!"

They were busy till bedtime with their cleaning. Jane wanted to scrub the floors; but Gilly vowed they were clean enough after all the brushing they had had. She eyed the kitchen floor doubtfully, and at last said it would have to do "for the present".

"Mr. Black hasn't left us a pail or scrubbing-brush or soap or floor-cloth, and the nearest water is a long way off, in Rushy Stream. I wonder how he managed. This floor must have been washed sometimes, one would think."

"There might be a well somewhere," said Gilly. "Let's look."

The well was found among the golden gorse bushes that were growing freely in the ruins. Its stout wooden cover was padlocked. Mr. Black was not going to allow anyone to fall in while he was away from the tower!

After they came back they mounted the

"My tower," said Gilly

ladder in the storeroom, unbolted the trap-door and pushed it back. Then they both climbed out on to the roof, which had a battlement running round it.

From the roof they had a wide view of countryside, sea and sky. Ireland was hidden from them behind far-away dim blue mists.

The Irish wind blew softly through Gilly's hair. He stood smiling to himself.

"What are you smiling at?" asked Jane. "What are you thinking about?"

"My tower," said Gilly. "Only my tower."

The Face With a Hundred Wrinkles

JANE and Gilly were glad that the next day was a Saturday and the next Monday a half-term holiday for Jane. They were busy all Saturday morning; for their best treasures had to be taken down to the tower in Gilly's wheelbarrow.

In the afternoon it rained so hard that Auntie Enid would not let them go out.

She still had not heard about the tower. They wanted the secret to be a grand surprise for Daddy's and Mummy's home-coming; but they knew that Auntie Enid, being a little forgetful, might not remember to say nothing about the tower when she was writing a letter.

Now what were they to do with a wet afternoon?

"Let's go up to the biggest attic. It has

"Heaps of old things that would be most useful"

heaps of old things that would be most useful for furnishing the tower. We will ask Daddy and Mummy to let us have them, since they are not being used any more."

"That's a good plan," said Gilly.

Till bedtime he and Jane were busy choosing what they needed. When they had made their choice, the attic appeared to have been visited by a tornado. At least, that is what Auntie Enid said when she went to find some odd ounces of wool she had put aside for a jumble sale.

"Jane and Gilly, what are you doing?" she asked.

"Only putting this lot ready to show Daddy and Mummy," said Jane. "We have a special secret reason. Please leave our things where they are, Auntie Enid! Please!"

"I hope your father and mother will come soon, that's all," said Auntie Enid.

"Such a scene of confusion! What have you got there, Gilly? Oh, that old picture. You may keep it if you like. It's mine."

"Thank you very, very much," said Gilly, and he went downstairs with the picture under his arm.

In their playroom, he showed his prize to Jane.

Against a wild, lonely landscape a great tower stood in all its strength under a dark and cloudy sky. A man was running with all his might to the tower, the door of which was open. At the foot of the picture these words were printed in gold letters:

THE NAME OF THE LORD IS A STRONG TOWER: THE RIGHTEOUS RUNNETH INTO IT AND IS SAFE.

"It's quite the most suitable picture we could have for hanging in our tower," said Jane. "We will put it up tomorrow afternoon when Auntie Enid is having her Sunday nap. That is, if this rain ever stops!"

There was no church on little Red Island; but on Sunday morning they were able to go to the mainland between showers.

Mr. David Jones's general store was close to the ferry, and next to it was the guest-house kept by his wife. All the summer visitors had gone home some weeks ago, and Mrs. Jones had said she should shut up her guest-house for the winter. But here she was, talking to an elderly woman who was plainly a guest.

"Might as well go to church, it will be something to pass the time on this wretched wet morning," the guest was saying, in disgusted tones. "Not that I'm much of a churchgoer. But you say the

church is only a step from the mainland
end of the ferry—and I don't want to
tramp about the island in pouring rain!"

"Oh, you'll enjoy the service!" said
Mrs. Jones. "Indeed, it is a very nice

service, and I only wish I could come too. But I can't, not with my Megan crying at home with toothache. Well, good-bye for the present, Mrs. Daunt."

"Is your little girl's name 'Megan'? So's mine. I never met a 'Megan' before," said Mrs. Daunt, not quite so crossly. She raised her head to give the sky another scowl, and then she stalked off to the ferry-boat, followed by Auntie Enid, Jane, and Gilly.

When they saw her face to face, Jane and Gilly thought they had never seen such a sad person. Her forehead was creased into a hundred wrinkles, her eyes stared grimly, and her lips made a tight, straight line.

Jane and Gilly enjoyed the service. Most of all they enjoyed the sermon, which had a text that even Auntie Enid did not know: *Uzziah built towers in the desert.*

King Uzziah also built towers in Jerusalem, said the preacher, but there was a special reason why he built towers in the desert where nobody lived. When a man

was lost in the wilderness or when he was being chased by his enemies, how thankful he must have been to catch sight of a strong tower waiting to shelter him in the hour of need.

Uzziah had been dead for nearly three thousand years and his towers were crumbled to dust long ago; but the memory of his deed would never die. It was written in the Bible for everyone to see.

Then the preacher said that God was Himself a tower—"a tower of salvation" —for those who had asked Him to forgive their sins for the Lord Jesus Christ's sake, and to take their whole lives into His keeping for ever and ever. When they were unhappy, lonely, frightened, or tempted to do wrong, they must remember to ask the Lord Jesus to be with them and to guide them in the right way. Doing that was like taking quick shelter in a mighty tower. Unseen walls of loving protection would be round them, keeping them safe.

Gilly remembered that when he meddled with the rocket in Porth Grisial, he had quite forgotten to ask that he might be kept from wrong-doing. In spite of that, he knew in his heart that his life did belong to the Lord Jesus.

"I have two towers, both mine," said Gilly to himself. "Jesus and the brown tower. Two!"

He looked across the aisle at Mrs. Daunt. Her face was gloomier than ever. It seemed to him that she had not liked the sermon about the tower.

Mrs. Daunt Visits the Tower

IN the afternoon the rain stopped. Jane and Gilly went down to the tower.

There were nails and picture-hooks in the wall. Jane mounted one of the wobbly chairs, and Gilly handed up the picture.

She had just jumped down when they saw the gloomy Mrs. Daunt coming along the path. Stopping by the open door, she peered in.

Jane and Gilly thought she was inquisitive; but she looked so dismal that they felt sorry for her.

"Would you like to come in and see our tower?" said Jane politely.

Gilly handed up the picture

"Oh, so it's your tower now, is it," said Mrs. Daunt.

"Yes, it is, but it wasn't always," Gilly answered. "Old Mr. Black had it, but he doesn't want it any longer."

At this moment the wobblier of the two chairs suddenly lost a leg and sat down in a heap on the floor. Jane was much ashamed.

"The chair isn't ours," she explained quickly. "It was left behind by Mr. Black. Our furniture will be coming down in a few days from our other house. I am afraid," said Jane, in a grown-up manner, "that you don't see our tower looking its best."

"Needs a good cleaning and doing over," said Mrs. Daunt, "but it's not bad, not bad at all."

"We've cleaned it!" cried Jane and Gilly indignantly.

"Umph!" was all Mrs. Daunt found to

say. She walked over to the windows and tried to open them, but the fastenings were too stiff. Then—"I'll have a sight of the upper floors if you've no objection," said she.

They led her to the bedroom and storeroom, and she stamped on the floor of each and approved of the result. "Ah! Good sound flooring," she said.

"Would you like to see the view from the roof?" asked Gilly.

"Not me!" said Mrs. Daunt.

They went downstairs.

"Where's the other house you mentioned?" said Mrs. Daunt. "Was the lady you were with your mum? What's your name?"

"No, that was our Aunt Enid," Jane answered. "Our name is Harcourt-Tudor. You can see our home over there among the trees."

"Looks like a castle."

"It is a castle, Castell Goch, the Red Castle."

Mrs. Daunt looked sour. "Your father's a big man, then?"

"No," said Gilly. "He's tall, but not big. Rather thin."

With a kind of snort, Mrs. Daunt said, "I mean, is he one of the high-ups? Important?"

Gilly turned to Jane. "Is Daddy important?" he asked.

"I s'pose so, I never thought about it. He's an ambassador—at least, he was until there was a civil war in a country called Karambodia, and he and Mummy had to come home. He's in London now, at the Foreign Office, but he and Mummy will be coming home this week, we don't know when. Why are you asking about him?"

"Never you mind," said Mrs. Daunt. Without another word, she whisked round and left the tower. They saw her walking down the track that led to the store and the guest-house.

"I think she was not at all polite," said Jane. "We asked her in so nicely, showed her everything and answered all her questions—and then she marches off like that without thanking us or even saying good afternoon! What do you think, Gilly?"

Gilly was puzzled too. "I think—I think—oh well, I think it's time to go home to tea!"

The kettle had not boiled when they arrived. To fill in the waiting-time, Gilly took out his *Life*. He wrote:

I have a tower, the strongest in the world and the best. I love my wonderful tower——

There he had to stop; for the teapot had been brought in.

CHAPTER
6

Prisoners in the Tower

EARLY on Monday morning Jane and Gilly found three or four of their schoolfellows waiting outside the tower. When Jane saw Megan Jones among them, she knew that Mrs. Daunt must have given their secret away.

Jane and Gilly could have done without their visitors, who spent the time dancing on the roof and poking their fingers into everything.

After an hour they went down to the store to buy potato crisps. Only Megan Jones stayed behind. She kept looking at her watch and smiling strangely.

"What's the matter?" Jane asked. "Is your tooth aching still?"

"No, it's better," Megan answered. "I've something to tell you, but I couldn't tell it till after ten o'clock. It's ten past now. That Mrs. Daunt!—I don't like her. She told Mother I had flat feet and ought to see a doctor. She came here yesterday, I know. I'll tell you why. She's after your tower!"

"No!" gasped Gilly.

"No!" gasped Jane.

"Oh yes, she is! She was as glum as glum yesterday after she'd been out walking. Mum and Dad couldn't think why. At night, she couldn't keep her troubles to herself any longer, and she got telling about her hard life. I lay on the sofa and listened. When her husband died she kept house for her son till he married a widow with six children. Then she had to turn out and be working housekeeper to old ladies. Five of them she had, one after the other, but none of them lasted long. It was most annoying, she said, the way she kept having to find a new job.

"When the fifth old lady died, she had saved enough money to have a little home of her own. She had her pension and some furniture, which a friend had stored for her in an empty garage. The question was, where could she find a house?

"And then she saw a piece in the paper about the seascape painter, Mr. Black, how he said he would never be going back to the tower where he had painted the most famous of his pictures.

"She knew he had taken possession of the tower, that's why she never tried to claim it before. It wouldn't have been any use, she said——"

"Claim it?" cried Jane and Gilly. *"Claim it?"*

"She says she's the last one left of all the families that claimed it long, long ago. Her grandfather lost a great deal of money forty years ago when he was trying to get the tower for himself, and he solemnly warned his children never to try again; for if you go to law you always lose your hard-earned cash. And they never did; but they kept the deeds and papers that he hoped would prove his claim. She's got them with her.

"So when she knew Mr. Black had cleared out, she thought here was her chance! But when she came, she found your father had given you the tower for a playhouse!

"Her name's Daunt—and she's easily daunted! She told Mum and Dad that she wouldn't lose her little bit of money by fighting for her rights. Your father was rich and powerful: she would just keep quiet and go away.

"Mum and Dad told her, over and over, that your father wasn't one to steal other people's towers. He was away from home, they said, and couldn't know that you had taken to playing down here. They begged her to see your Auntie Enid and to stop on a few days so that she could have a talk with your Dad. But no, she wouldn't hear of it! She cried and carried on, but nothing would make her change her mind about leaving this morning by the ten o'clock bus.—Gilly, Jane! Where are you going?"

"Going to find Mrs. Daunt," said Gilly miserably. "I thought the tower was mine, but it isn't. I must tell her."

Megan barred the way.

"Don't be so daft, boy! Let her go!—

then you'll be as safe as houses! We don't know where she lives; for she didn't write beforehand, and I'm almost certain Mum forgot to ask her to sign her name in the visitors' book. Once she's gone from Red Island, she's gone for ever and you can keep your tower."

"It isn't my tower any more, and I can't!"

"You little stupid, you can't catch her now! I tell you, it's twenty past ten."

"Your watch is always going wrong. If we're quick, the bus may still be there. Move out, Megan!"

Megan did move out, but not in the way Gilly expected. With one catlike bound, she sprang out of the tower and slammed the door on him and Jane. They heard the key turn in the lock.

"No, you don't!" she shouted. "If you

don't want this tower, me and the other kids do. It's gorgy! too good to lose— and we'll stand up for our rights! We

"Stop, stop," yelled Gilly and Jane

don't want her here, with a face to turn the cream sour. Telling Mum I had flat feet, indeed! I'll keep you locked up till she's gone to wherever she's going. See?"

Gilly didn't answer. "The windows, Jane! Quick!"

He and Jane wrestled with the stiff catches that Mrs. Daunt could not move. They hurt their fingers and pinched their thumbs, and all the while the minutes were flying by faster, faster.

Outside the tower Megan laughed and capered. She was feeling triumphant when suddenly one of the windows yielded. It swung open, and Gilly and Jane came tumbling through.

Megan gave a whoop of dismay and ran off, calling, "Don't you be meanies, don't you split on me!"

Gilly and Jane did not even hear her. They were running as they had never run before, waving to the ferry to stop for them.

It had begun to cross the channel; but the ferryman obligingly chugged back again.

Now they were on the mainland, running, running.

The bus was moving off. "Stop, stop, STOP!" yelled Gilly and Jane.

The bus halted. Jane jumped on to the step, Gilly after her.

7

The Wonderful Tower

MRS. DAUNT was in the bus, gloomier than ever. She had a suitcase and a bulgy black handbag.

"Mrs. Daunt, come out! It's all a mistake. Daddy doesn't know Mr. Black has gone away. We didn't know the tower was yours. Come out!"

They couldn't make Mrs. Daunt understand at first, they were talking so fast that they jumbled their words together. When she did understand, she did not know whether to believe what they said. The bus conductor grew tired of waiting.

"Look, lady," he said, "are you going to the railway station or are you not?"

"I am not," said Mrs. Daunt.

The bus rumbled off without her.

Jane and Gilly had to explain once more. Jane did most of the explaining; for Gilly was too sad to talk.

Mrs. Daunt asked only one question: "Who told you about me?"

"Megan Jones," said Jane.

"Megan is a very good girl. I shall give her a little something," said Mrs. Daunt.

Jane and Gilly did not think Megan deserved a little anything. But they kept their thoughts to themselves.

A change for the better had already come over Mrs. Daunt. She held her head proudly like a property-owner, and she stepped along briskly, not looking nearly so wrinkled and old.

At the guest-house she took the suitcase that Jane and Gilly had been helping to carry, and went to tell Mrs. Jones

Jane wrote down the measurements

that she would be staying there until her furniture arrived. "Well now, it's glad I am to hear it!" said Mrs. Jones.

Everybody was glad save Gilly. Jane was a little sorry to lose the tower; but she forgot her sorrow in the interest of working for the tower's new owner.

They went back to it with Mrs. Daunt, out of whose bulgy black handbag came pencil, paper, tape measure. It was Jane who wrote down the measurements for window curtains, carpets, and rugs, and Jane who ran backwards and forwards to the store with lists of the things that Mrs. Daunt would need.

Meanwhile Gilly kept on taking wheel-barrow-loads of his and Jane's possessions back to the Castle. Everything went home, down to the broom and the duster that had been yellow and was now black.

The picture was left till the last.

When he came to fetch it, Jane had

gone down to the shop again. Mrs. Daunt was alone.

She was standing before the picture, looking at the man running towards the

Gilly saw she had tears in her eyes

tower. Gilly saw she had tears in her eyes.

He could not think why she should cry now. Here she was, safe in his own dear tower for the rest of her days! All her troubles were over—what had she to cry for?

There was no one to tell him that Mrs. Daunt was crying because she had heard a sermon that told her she had made her life hard and lonely by shutting the Lord Jesus out of it. She had not wanted any of the good things He had to offer, not even His best gift of Himself, the Tower of Salvation.

Gilly wanted to do something kind, to comfort her.

"Would you like to keep that picture?" he asked. "It's mine, but it seems to belong here."

Mrs. Daunt dried her eyes. "There's nothing I'd like better," she said.

"It's a picture worth having. Thank you."

Gilly went away with empty barrow. At home, he took out his *Life*. Now that the tower was lost to him for ever, he would have to cross out the last two sentences he had written.

He read them over again:

I have a tower, the strongest in the world and the best. I love my wonderful tower——

"Why," said Gilly, "I needn't scratch out those sentences after all. They are true with a different kind of true. I've lost one of my two towers, but not the other. I still have a wonderful Tower!"